When a hurricane blew through the swampy Everglades, two little eggs were swept from their nests and floated down the river. After the storm was over, the eggs hatched side by side in the soft, sweet grass of the riverbank. And that is how an alligator named Spike and a snowy egret named Mike came to live together as brothers in a very special place known as Cypress Glade.

Fairest of All

By MARY PACKARD

Illustrations based on characters created
and designed by Lisa McCue

 CHILDRENS PRESS®

CHICAGO

Text © 1993 Nancy Hall, Inc. Illustrations © 1993 Lisa McCue. All rights reserved.
Printed in the United States of America. Published by Grolier Direct Marketing, Danbury, Connecticut.
Drawings by Meryl Henderson. Paintings by Toni Scribner.
Design by Antler & Baldwin Group. ISBN 0-516-00826-9
A SPIKE n MIKE BOOK PRINTED ON RECYCLED PAPER

All of Cypress Glade was buzzing with excitement! Spike the alligator and Mike the bird were flying their kite when they heard the big news.

"Someone famous is coming to Cypress Glade!" announced Scarlett the flamingo, yanking on the kite string to get their attention.

"Oh?" asked Spike, trying to keep the kite from dipping. "Who's coming?"

"None other than Preston Peacock!" declared Scarlett.

"You mean the famous movie star?" asked Mike.

"Yes!" squealed Scarlett. "And he's coming to stay at my house! Tomorrow!"

"That is news!" cried Spike and Mike together, forgetting all about their kite.

"Preston's mother and my grandmother are old friends," continued Scarlett. "Preston wanted a vacation, so his mother suggested he come here!"

"Wow!" cried Spike. "A movie star! In Cypress Glade!"

"I know!" cried Scarlett. "Isn't it wonderful? Let's invite all our friends over to my house tomorrow. Then Preston can meet everyone, and everyone can meet him."

"Great idea!" agreed Spike.

"We'll tell the others," said Mike, and off they went to spread the news.

No one in the swamp had ever actually met a peacock before. But they had all seen pictures of Preston. In fact he had been on the cover of every magazine and newspaper in the swamp!

Now, for the first time ever, they were going to meet a real, live peacock, and a movie star, too. Of course they would stop by Scarlett's house first thing tomorrow!

The next day Scarlett woke up bright and early. She needed time to get ready for her special guest.

"Now, let's see, which bow should I wear?" she wondered, walking toward the mirror. "Yuk!" she yelled, when she saw herself in the glass. For the first time in her life, Scarlett did not like her own reflection.

"Pink is so boring," she said to herself. "If only my feathers were more colorful, like Preston's."

Suddenly an idea popped into her head. "I know," she said. "I'll touch up my feathers with paint from my paint set."

Scarlett went to work. She put a little blue paint here and a little green paint there, and then a few dabs of gold and purple in all the right places.

"Now I look much prettier," she said, quite pleased with herself. "I'll bet Preston will think so, too!"

Meanwhile, at their house, Spike and Mike were also fussing over their reflections.

"I don't look special enough to meet a peacock," worried Mike. "My feathers are too short and too plain. Maybe some streamers would help."

Mike soon found some colorful ribbons and began to weave them through his feathers. Spike looked on in admiration.

"It's not going to be easy to make an alligator look fancy," Spike thought in despair. Then he had a brilliant idea.

"Sparkles are what I need!" cried Spike, in a sudden burst of inspiration. He handed his brother some paste and a jar of glitter. "Mike, would you mind putting some of this on my tail?"

In fact, all of Scarlett's friends had the same thought that morning. They wanted to look good for Preston. So they, too, went to a lot of trouble to make themselves look fancier.

The frog brothers Gumbo and Jumbo made necklaces out of water lilies and shells. Sass and Frass, two playful raccoons, turned pine cones into crowns. Bo the bunny made a beautiful hat from the colorful vegetables in his garden.

By noon that day, everyone had gathered at Scarlett's house. Together, they waited nervously for the famous peacock to arrive.

Finally there was a knock at the door. Scarlett quickly opened it, and in walked Preston Peacock.

"Welcome to Cypress Glade, Mr. Peacock," said Scarlett, her voice trembling with excitement. "I'm Scarlett, and these are my friends."

"I'm delighted to meet you," said the beautiful bird. "Please, call me Peak. All my friends do."

"Have you ever seen anyone so handsome?" Scarlett whispered to Spike. "I wish he would show us that special thing he does with his feathers."

Finally she got up the courage to ask.

"You mean this?" asked Peak, arranging his tail feathers in a beautiful fan.

Everyone gasped when they saw it.

Suddenly the room was quiet. All anyone could do was stare.

"It's really no big deal," said Peak modestly. "Any peacock can do it."

"I'd love to paint your picture someday," said Scarlett, breaking the silence.

"May I have your autograph?" asked Bo.

All the attention was making Peak uncomfortable. He wished everyone would stop staring at him. He wished they would relax and take off those silly decorations. Most of all, he wished someone would offer to show him the swamp!

Besides Peak, Dixie Otter was the only guest at Scarlett's party who was not wearing any special decorations. In fact she couldn't understand what all the fuss was about. "Peacocks are just like anyone else, aren't they?" thought Dixie.

"How would you like to go to the pond and play on my vine swing?" she asked Peak.

"I sure would!" the peacock quickly replied. "Why don't we all go together?"

The others could hardly believe their ears.

"Why would Peak want to play on a swing?" they wondered. "What if his beautiful feathers got all messed up?"

But the others followed Dixie and Peak to the pond anyway. They walked very slowly, so as not to mess up their decorations. Then they watched as Dixie and Peak took turns jumping into the water from the vine swing.

"Whee! This is fun!" cried Peak.

"Are you sure you don't want to join us?" Dixie called to the others.

"Well . . . okay," said Spike, who loved to play more than anything. One by one the others jumped in the water. Soon they were all having so much fun that they forgot about their decorations.

Sass and Frass's crowns fell off as soon as they hit the water.

Mike's ribbons got soaked.

Spike's glitter rubbed off.

Gumbo and Jumbo's necklaces wilted.

Bo's hat got all soggy.

And Scarlett's paint dripped all over the ground.

After a while they all came out of the pond, breathless
and ready for a snack.

As she was drying off, Scarlett looked at her reflection
in the water. "I look so plain now," she thought.

The others stared sadly at their reflections, too.

"Why so glum?" asked Peak. "I thought we were having fun."

"It's just that we look so ordinary now!" exclaimed Scarlett. "We went to a lot of trouble to make ourselves look as special as you, and now look at us!"

"To tell you the truth," said Peak. "I think you look much nicer without those silly decorations!"

"You do?" questioned Mike.

"Of course I do," said the peacock. "Who cares how you look? It's who you are inside that counts!"

"But you are so beautiful," said Spike. "We wanted to be beautiful, too."

"I'll let you in on a secret," said Peak. "Beauty isn't all it's cracked up to be. I don't always like it when people stare at me or give me special treatment. And besides, I came to Cypress Glade to have a good time. I had heard that there were a lot of fun things to do here. But until Dixie came along, I was beginning to think I was in the wrong place!"

"We just wanted you to like us," said Scarlett.

"And I wanted you to like me, too," said Peak, "but not because of how I look. I wanted you to like me for who I am."

"Oh, we do," said Scarlett. "You're the best!"

"Thanks," laughed Peak. "So what do you say we really get to be friends?" he asked, taking hold of the vine swing.

"Last one in is a rotten egg!" he called out, just before he hit the water with a big splash.

Let's Talk About It

In *Fairest of All*, Preston Peacock came to Cypress Glade for a vacation. "Peak" was a movie star, and he was the first peacock to visit the swamp. Scarlett and her friends wanted to impress Peak, so they put on decorations to make themselves look fancy.

To everyone's surprise, Peak did not like the decorations. He wished Scarlett and her friends would just be themselves. And he wished they would like him for who he was, too, not just for how he looked. Peak explained that being beautiful on the outside is not as important as being beautiful on the inside.

The characters in Cypress Glade were so busy worrying about how they looked, they forgot about all the things that make them who they are. For example, Spike is friendly, and Mike likes adventure. These are the things that really make them special—not how they look or any decorations they wear.

Think about your best friend. What are some of the things you like about him or her? Is your friend kind? smart? funny? What do you think your friend likes about you? Do you agree with Peak that *who you are* is more important than *how you look*?

Cards That Care

Some cards tell a friend "Happy Birthday" or "Get Well Soon." Other cards tell a friend you think he or she is special. Here is a card you can make for your best friend.

This is what you'll need:
1 piece of construction paper
markers or crayons

Fold the piece of construction paper in half to make a card. (See the picture.) On the front of the card, draw a symbol that tells what makes your friend special. Think of your own symbol or use one of these:

smart, talented   strong   friendly   kind, caring

Color in the symbol. Then open the card and write a message telling your friend why he or she is special. Sign your name under the message. Give the card to your friend the next time you see him or her.

SALTY
LAGOON

SCARLETT'S
HOUSE

SLINK'S
HOLE

SASS
AND
FRASS'S
HOUSE

MULBERRY
MARSH

MOONFLOWER
MEADOW

FIDDLESTICKS
DAM

BLOSSOM'S
LODGE

DIXIE'S
DEN

MINNOW
CREEK

LOBLOLLY
POND

PERCY'S
HOUSE

GLADE

DUMP